little Miss Wise

by Roger Hargreaves

PSS!
PRICE STERN SLOAN

Little Miss Wise was as wise as an owl.

Possibly two owls.

Being so wise and sensible meant that Little
Miss Wise brushed her teeth every day,
made her bed every day,
tidied her house every day,
and did lots of other wise and sensible things.

If you are as wise as Little Miss Wise, you'll know
just what kind of other things she did.

Little Miss Wise liked to go for a walk every day.

A walk that was neither too long, nor too short.

A walk that was wise and sensible.

Or sensible and wise, if you prefer.

On her walks she often met other people.

People who were not quite so wise.

And sometimes, people who were very, very unwise.

Last Monday she met Little Miss Naughty.

"Come and jump in the puddles!" cried Little Miss Naughty, with a naughty gleam in her eye.

But Little Miss Wise, being wise, refused.

She didn't want to get HER feet wet.

On Tuesday she met Little Miss Greedy, who was carrying an enormous cake filled with cream and smothered with pink icing.

"Would you like some of this?"
asked Little Miss Greedy.

Little Miss Wise refused.

She didn't want an upset stomach.

On Wednesday Little Miss Wise refused to get into Mr. Busy's race car.

She didn't want to have an accident.

On Thursday she refused to go into
Mr. Messy's house.

"If I go into his house I will get dirty,"
she said to herself.

But she didn't say anything to Mr. Messy.

She didn't want to hurt his feelings.

On Friday she refused to play tennis with Mr. Silly.

There's nothing silly about that, is there?

By Saturday, Little Miss Wise was feeling unhappy.

"If I keep saying 'no' all the time, I'll upset everybody and I won't have any friends left," she said to herself.

She thought long and hard about the problem, and being the wise and sensible person she is, she came up with an answer.

"From now on, I will say 'yes' to everything."

On Sunday, while she was out on one of her wise and sensible walks—or sensible and wise walks, if you prefer—Little Miss Wise met Mr. Mischief.

He was carrying a package.

"Please accept this small present," he said to her.

"N—" began Little Miss Wise, but then she remembered her decision.

"Yes! Thank you!" she cried.

She took the package.

And Mr. Mischief skipped off with a mischievous grin on his face.

Little Miss Wise opened the package.

"Ahhh-CHOOO!" she sneezed.

Then she sneezed again.

And she sneezed, and sneezed, and sneezed all day long.

She used 199 handkerchiefs.

Mr. Mischief's present was sneezing powder!

Today is Monday and Little Miss Wise has stopped sneezing.

She is on one of her wise and sensible walks—or sensible and wise walks, if you prefer—and she has met Mr. Nonsense.

"Would you like a ride in my airplane?" he asks.

"N—" Little Miss Wise starts to say.

But then she changes her mind and exclaims: "Oh, yes please!"

You think she is being very unwise, don't you? You think she should have learned her lesson by now, don't you?

Well, she's safe this time.

Because Mr. Nonsense's airplane doesn't have any wings, or an engine, or even wheels.

It's just a doormat.

Have you ever heard of such nonsense?

DATE DUE

JUN. 19 1998		APR 0 2 2008
SEP. 02 199	FEB 19 2000	SEP 29 2010
SEP. 11 1998	NOV 2 2 2000	MAY 2 4 2011
SEP. 29 1998		
NOV. 25 1998	DEC 26 2001	
FEB. 02 1999	JUN 28 2005	
MAR 27 1993	DEC 17 2005	
APR. 13 1993	OCT 2 4 2006	
MAY 22 1993	APR 0 2 2007	